Dear Parent:
Your child's love of reading starts here!

Every child learns to read in a different way and at his or her own speed. Some go back and forth between reading levels and read favorite books again and again. Others read through each level in order. You can help your young reader improve and become more confident by encouraging his or her own interests and abilities. From books your child reads with you to the first books he or she reads alone, there are I Can Read Books for every stage of reading:

SHARED READING
Basic language, word repetition, and whimsical illustrations, ideal for sharing with your emergent reader

BEGINNING READING
Short sentences, familiar words, and simple concepts for children eager to read on their own

READING WITH HELP
Engaging stories, longer sentences, and language play for developing readers

READING ALONE
Complex plots, challenging vocabulary, and high-interest topics for the independent reader

ADVANCED READING
Short paragraphs, chapters, and exciting themes for the perfect bridge to chapter books

I Can Read Books have introduced children to the joy of reading since 1957. Featuring award-winning authors and illustrators and a fabulous cast of beloved characters, I Can Read Books set the standard for beginning readers.

A lifetime of discovery begins with the magical words "I Can Read!"

Visit www.icanread.com for information
on enriching your child's reading experience.

I Can Read® is a trademark of HarperCollins Publishers.

Justice League: I Am Green Lantern
Copyright © 2013 DC Comics.
JUSTICE LEAGUE and all related characters and elements are trademarks of and © DC Comics.
(s13)

HARP29334
Printed in the United States of America. No part of this book may be used or reproduced in any manner whatsoever without written permission except in the case of brief quotations embodied in critical articles and reviews. For information address HarperCollins Children's Books, a division of HarperCollins Publishers, 195 Broadway, New York, NY 10007.
www.icanread.com

Library of congress catalog card number: 2013931377
ISBN 978-0-06-221006-7
Book design by John Sazaklis

15 16 17 18   PC/WOR   10 9 8 7 6   ❖   First Edition

I Can Read!

READING 2 WITH HELP

JUSTICE LEAGUE

I Am
Green
Lantern

by Ray Santos
pictures by Steven E. Gordon
colors by Eric A. Gordon

HARPER
An Imprint of HarperCollinsPublishers

The Green Lantern Corps

protects the universe.

Each Green Lantern is in

charge of a different sector.

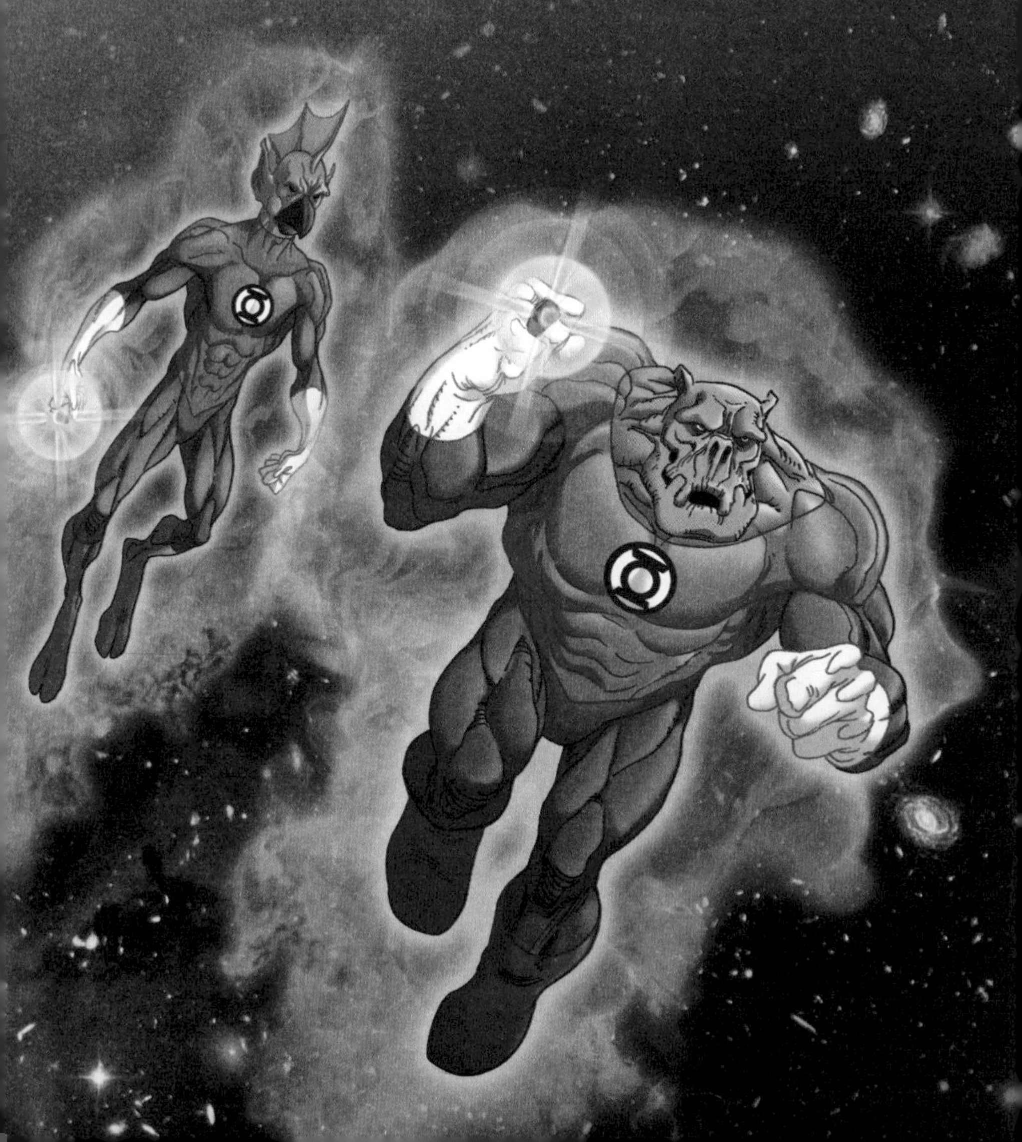

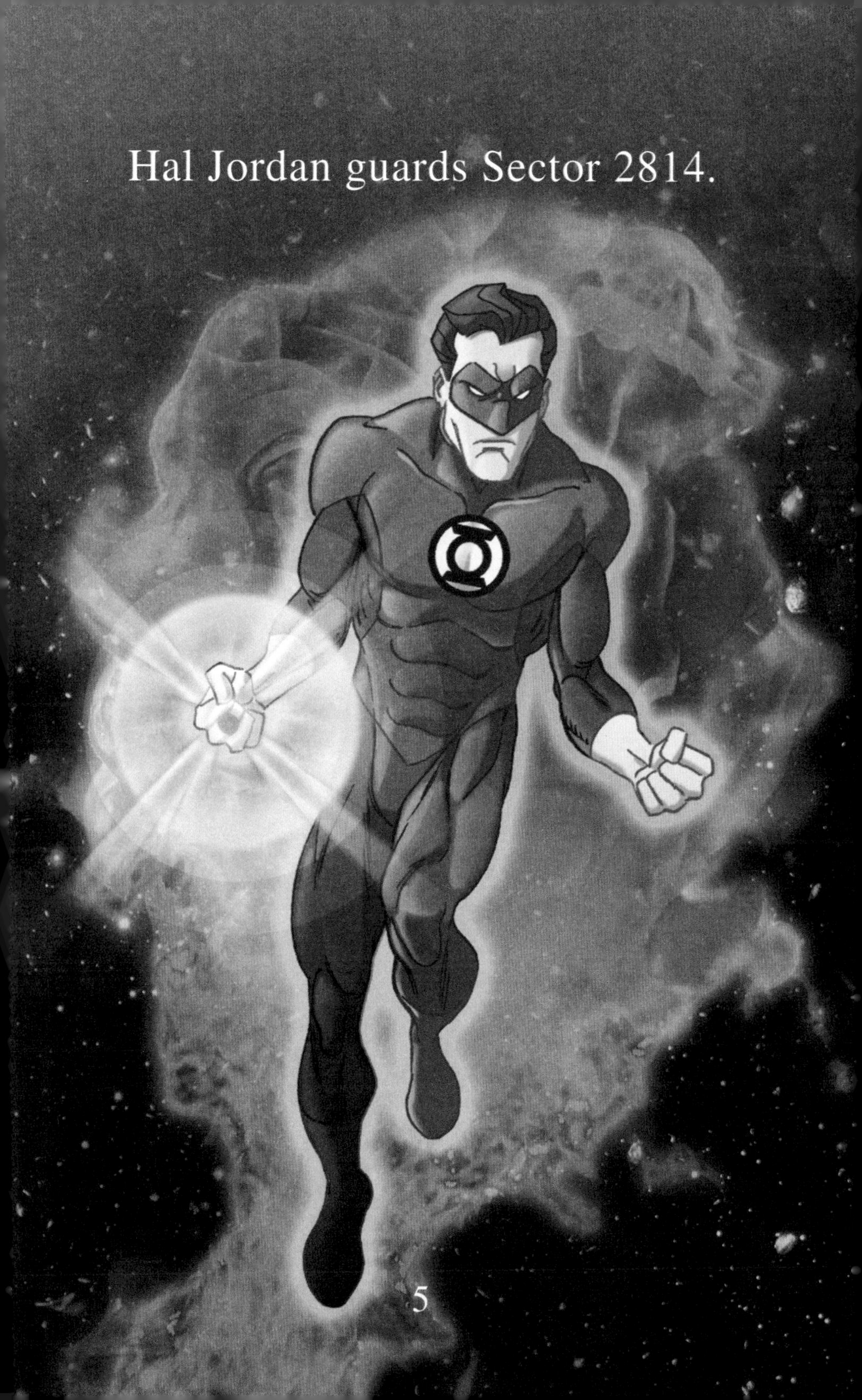

Hal Jordan guards Sector 2814.

The planet Earth is in Sector 2814.

It is Hal's job

to make sure no aliens attack Earth

or any other planet in his sector.

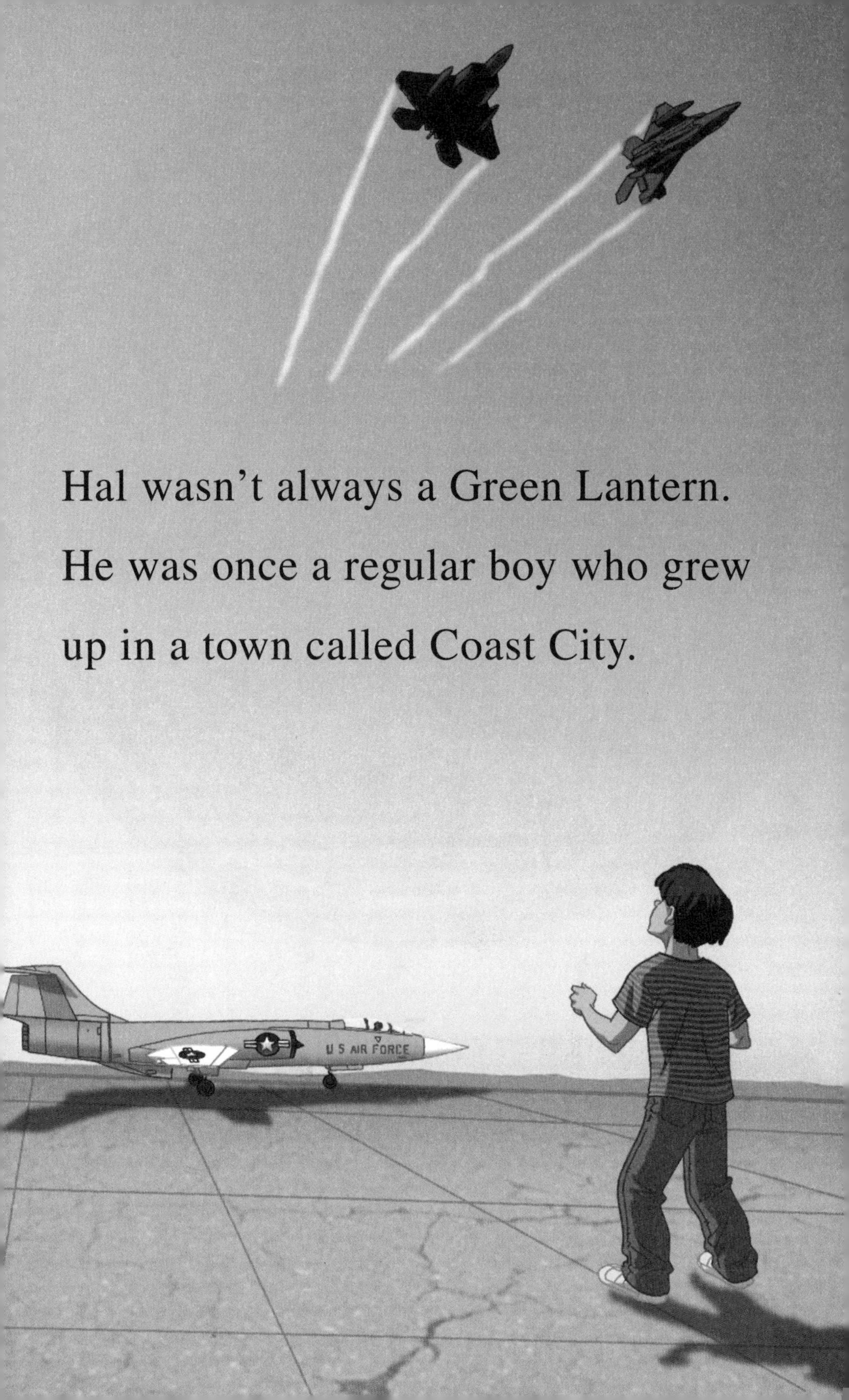
U S AIR FORCE

Hal wasn't always a Green Lantern. He was once a regular boy who grew up in a town called Coast City.

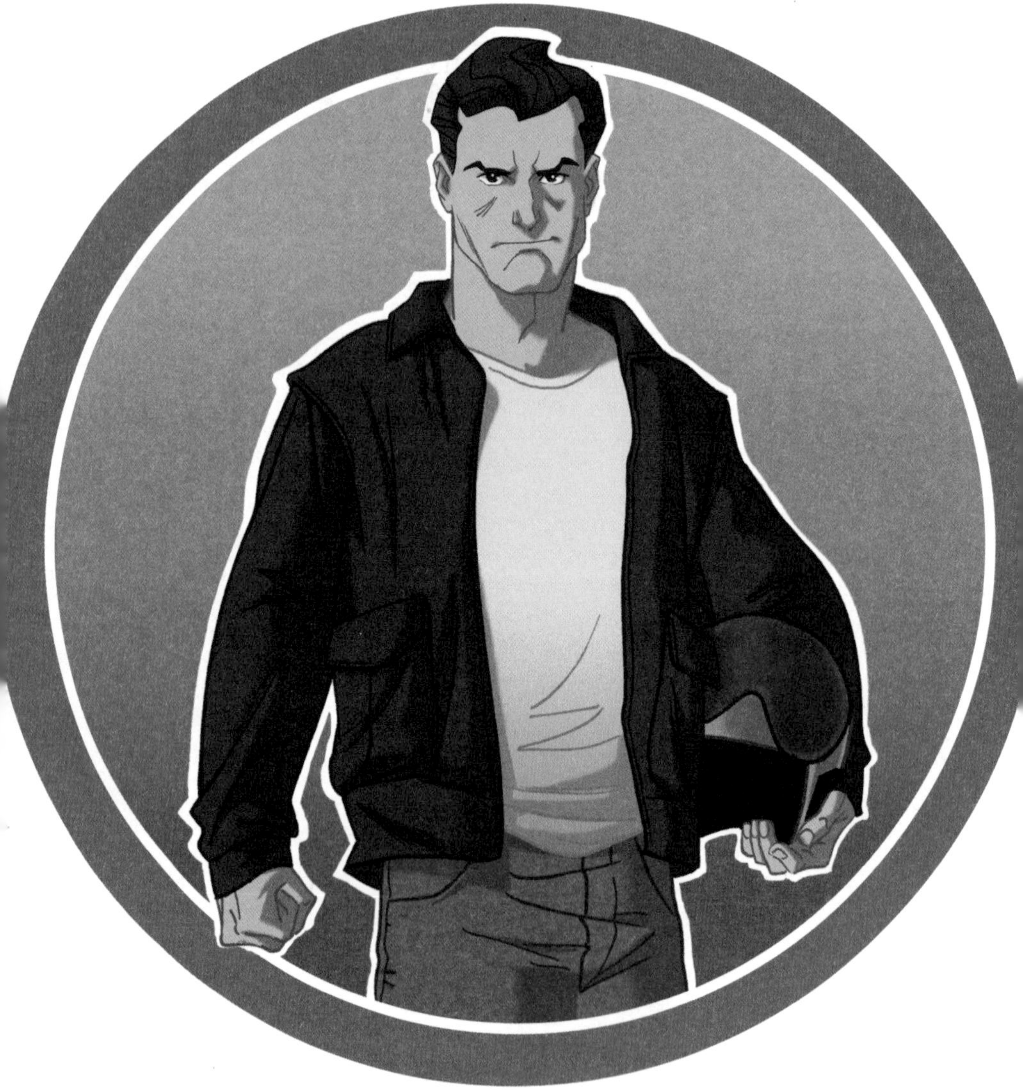

When he was older,
Hal became a test pilot,
just like his father had been.

It was a dangerous job,

but he wasn't afraid.

Hal wasn't afraid of anything.

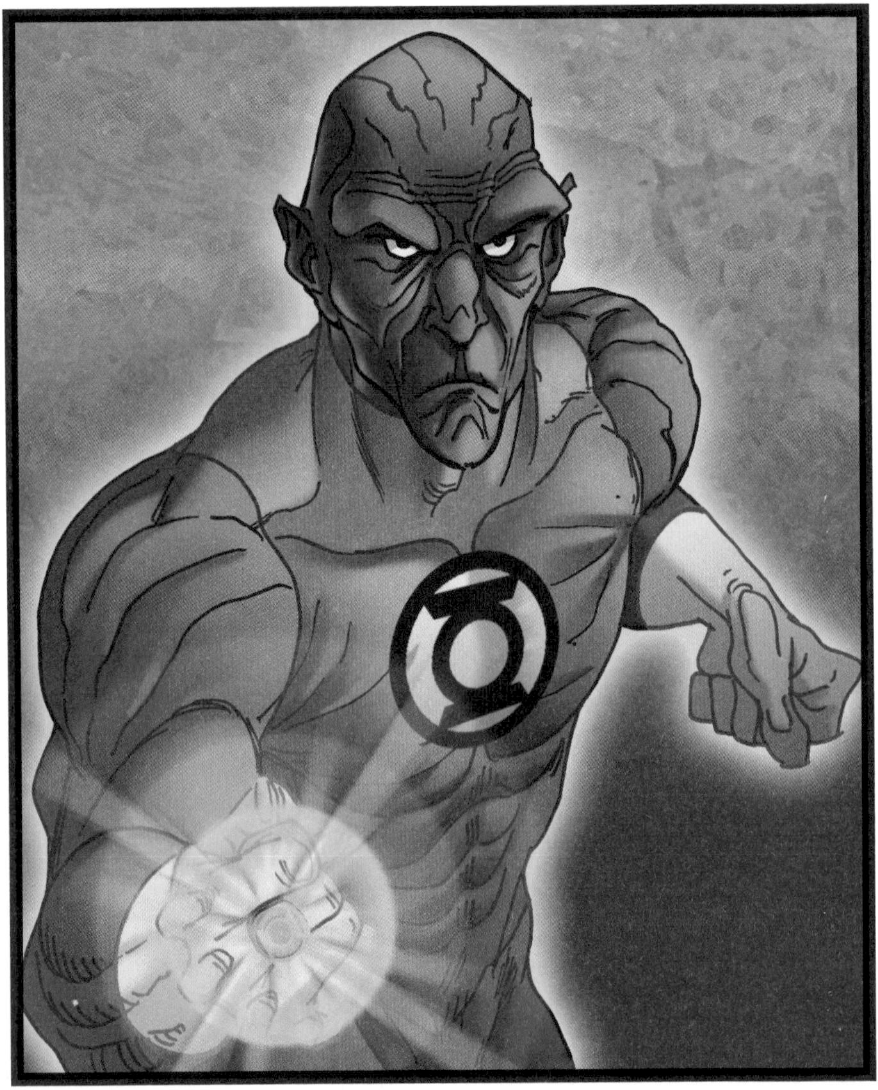

Before Hal, Sector 2814's Green Lantern was an alien named Abin Sur.

He had protected the area for a long time.

Abin Sur got into a bad fight,
and his spaceship was damaged.
It was headed on a crash course
with Earth, and he couldn't stop it.

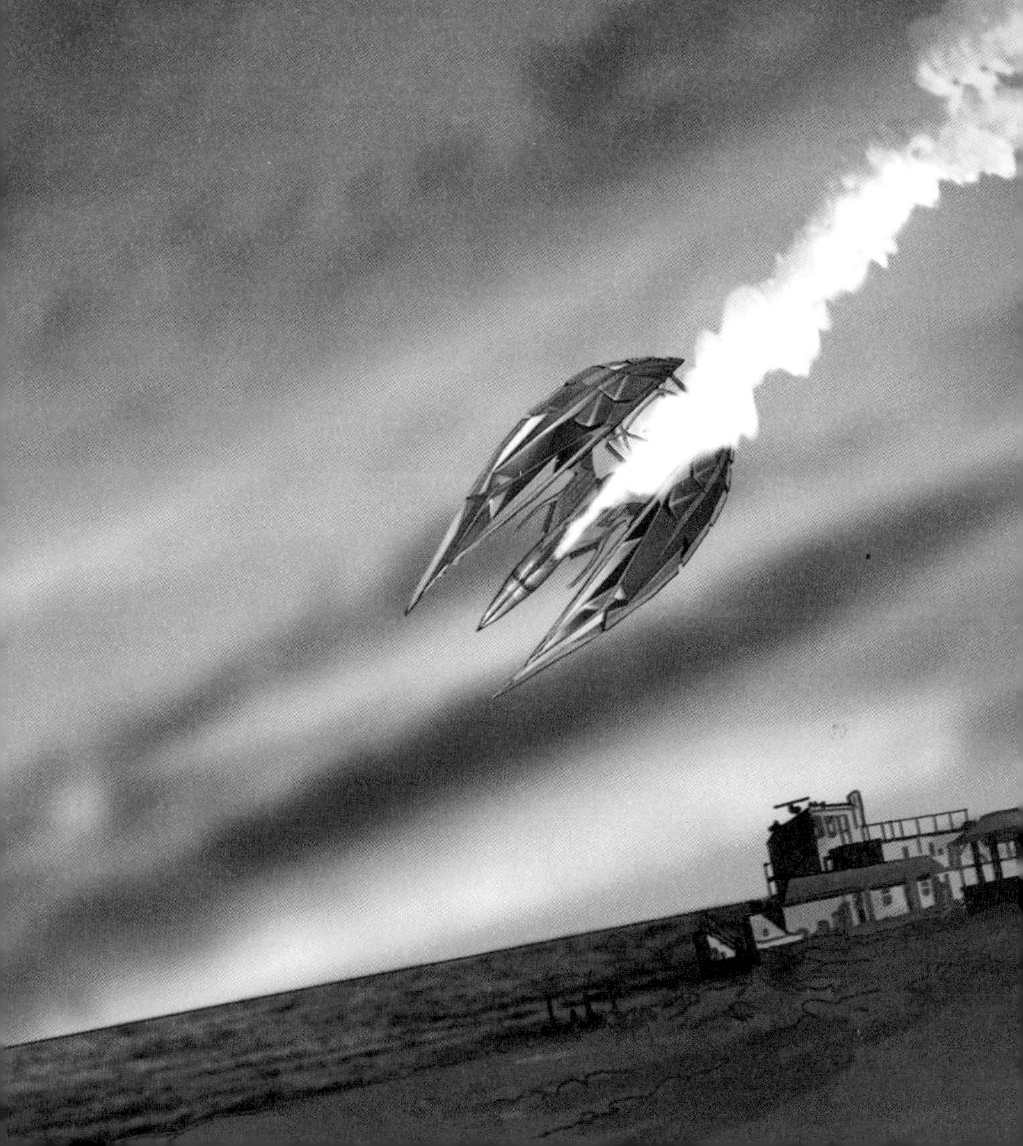

Abin Sur knew that he
wouldn't survive the crash.
A new Green Lantern
had to be found.
He used his Green Lantern
power ring to find someone
who was worthy.

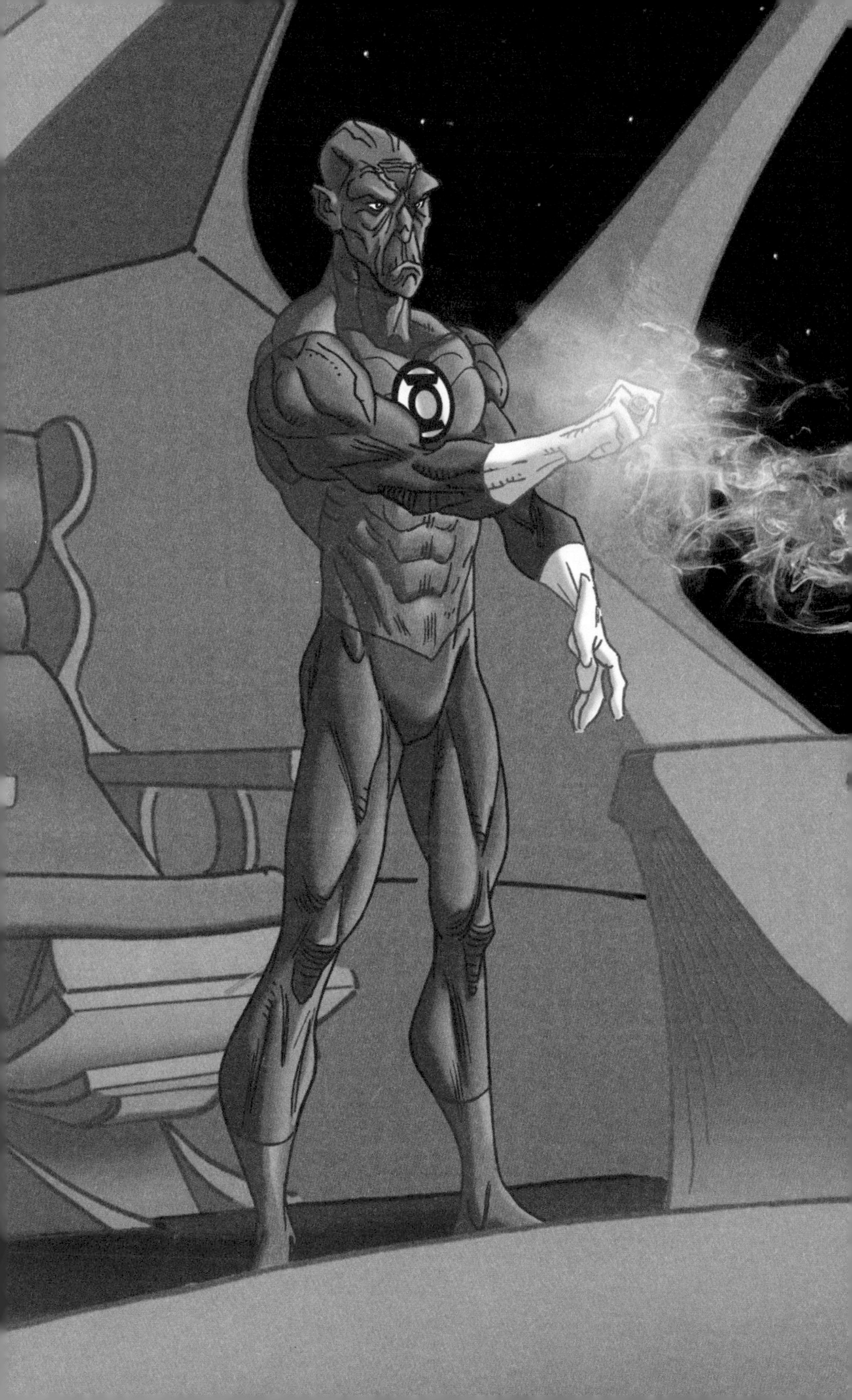

Hal saw Abin Sur's ship crashing to Earth.
Something called him to the crash site.
He knew that he had to go there.
As soon as Hal saw the crashed ship,
he ran over to it.

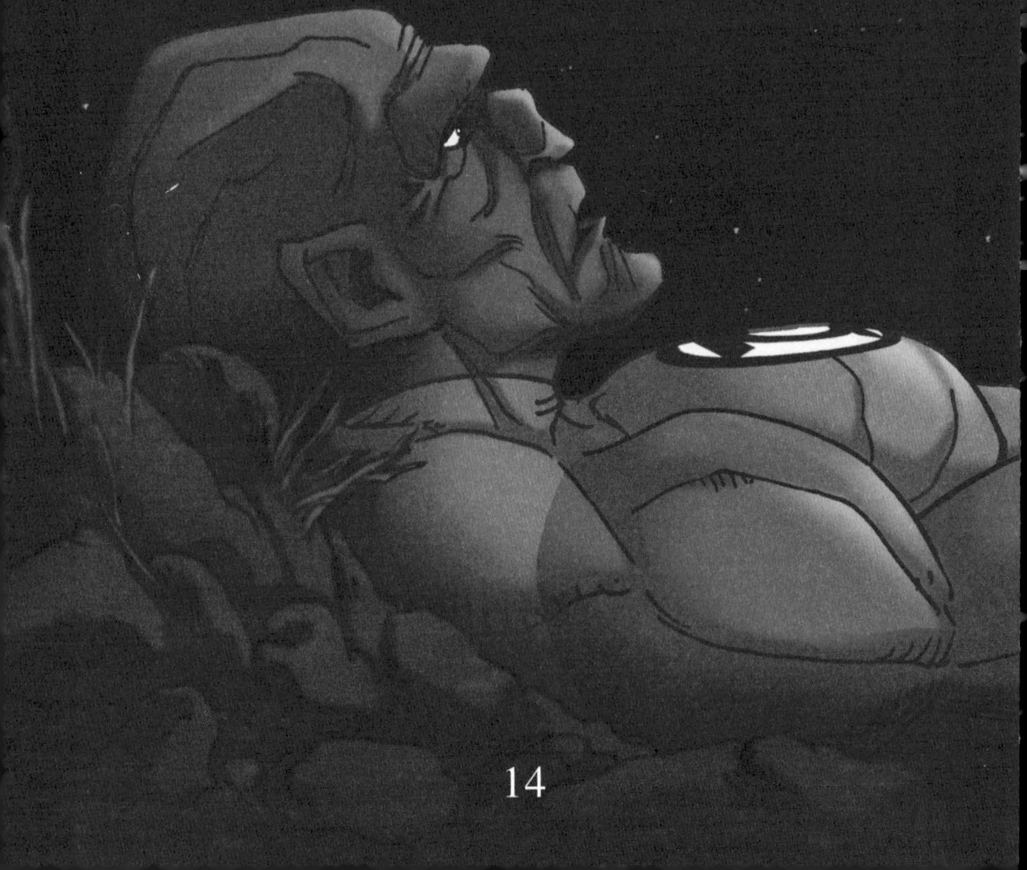

He had never seen a spaceship
or an alien before, but he wasn't scared.

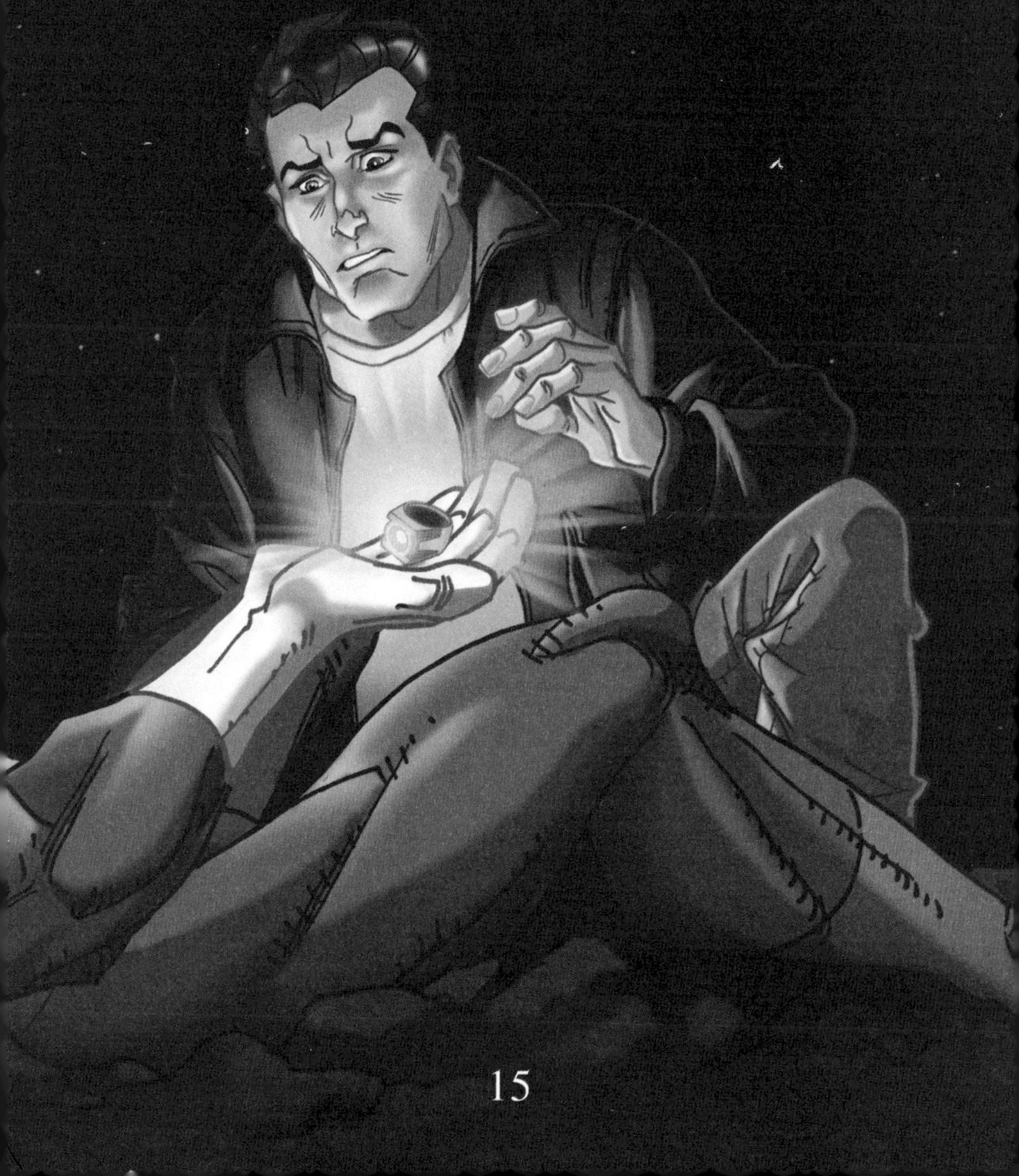

"The ring has chosen you,"
the alien said.
Abin Sur held out his
Green Lantern power ring.
"Because you are a person
who can overcome great fear,"
Abin Sur added.
The ring floated through the air to Hal.

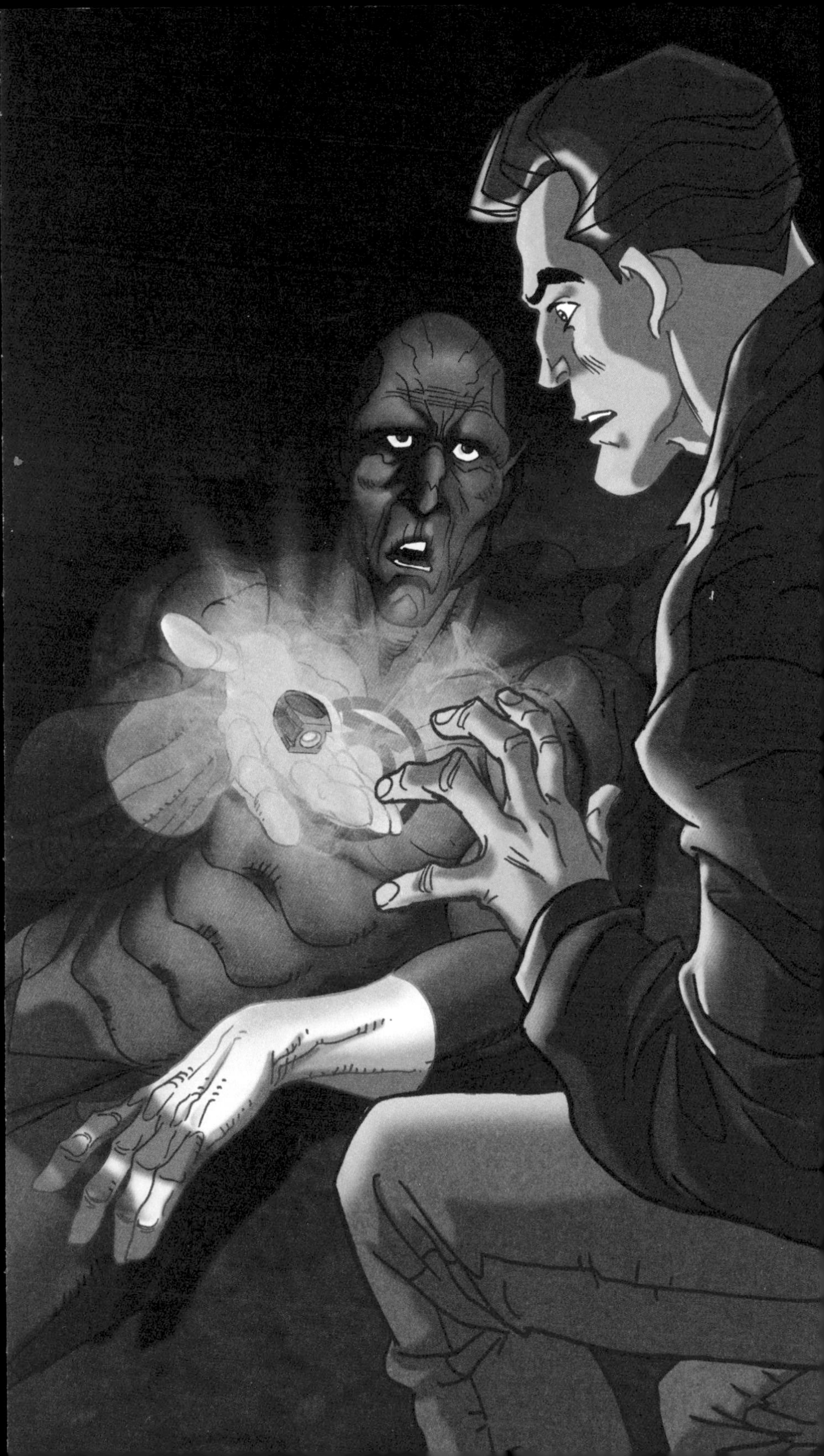

Hal put the ring on his finger,

and his clothes turned into

a Green Lantern uniform.

"Welcome to the Green Lantern Corps,"

Abin Sur said to him.

"Your ring is what gives you

your powers," the alien said.

"Its green energy can form

into anything you can imagine."

He told Hal that fear was the only

thing that could defeat a Green Lantern.

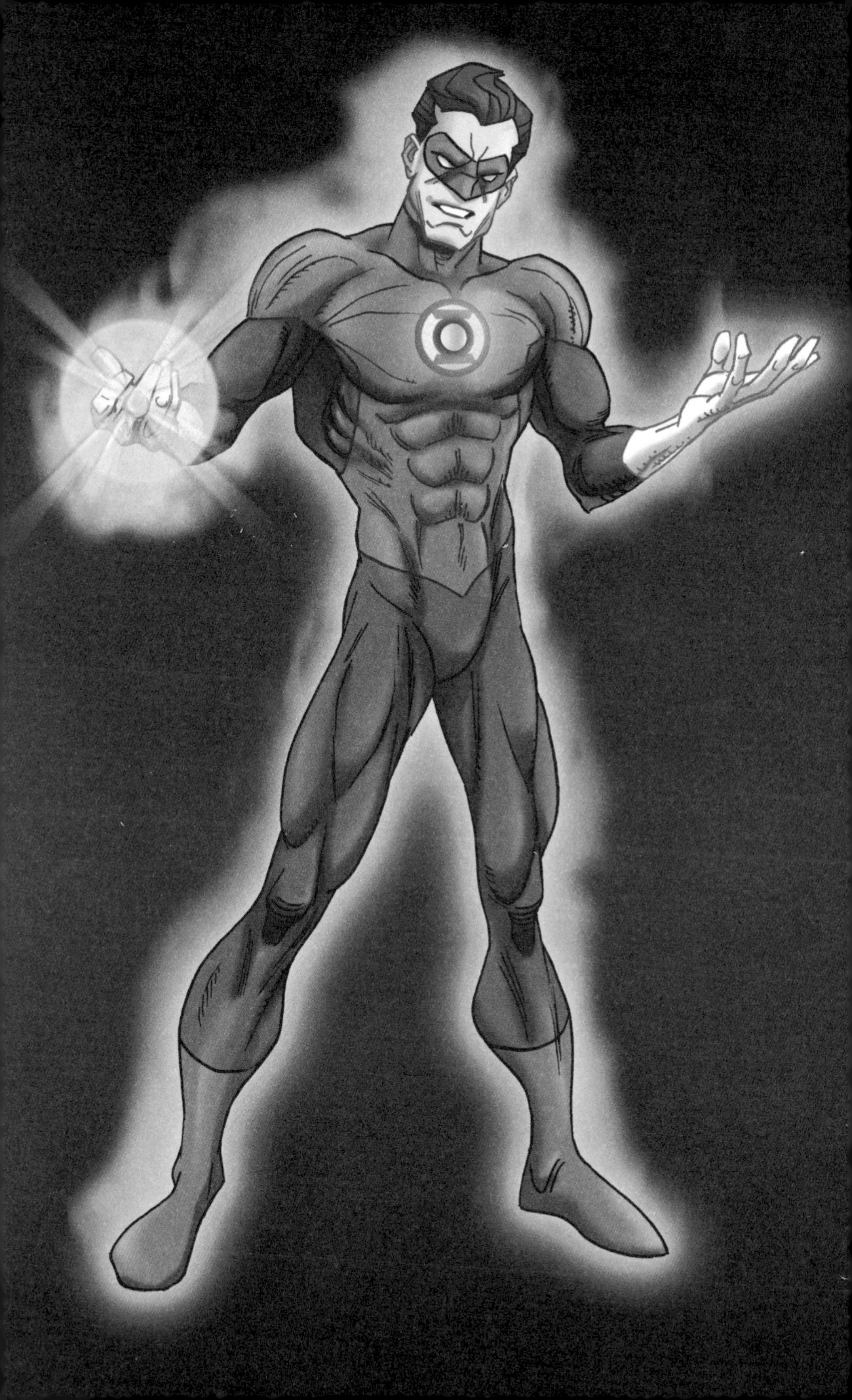

The ring took Hal to the
Green Lantern home world of Oa.

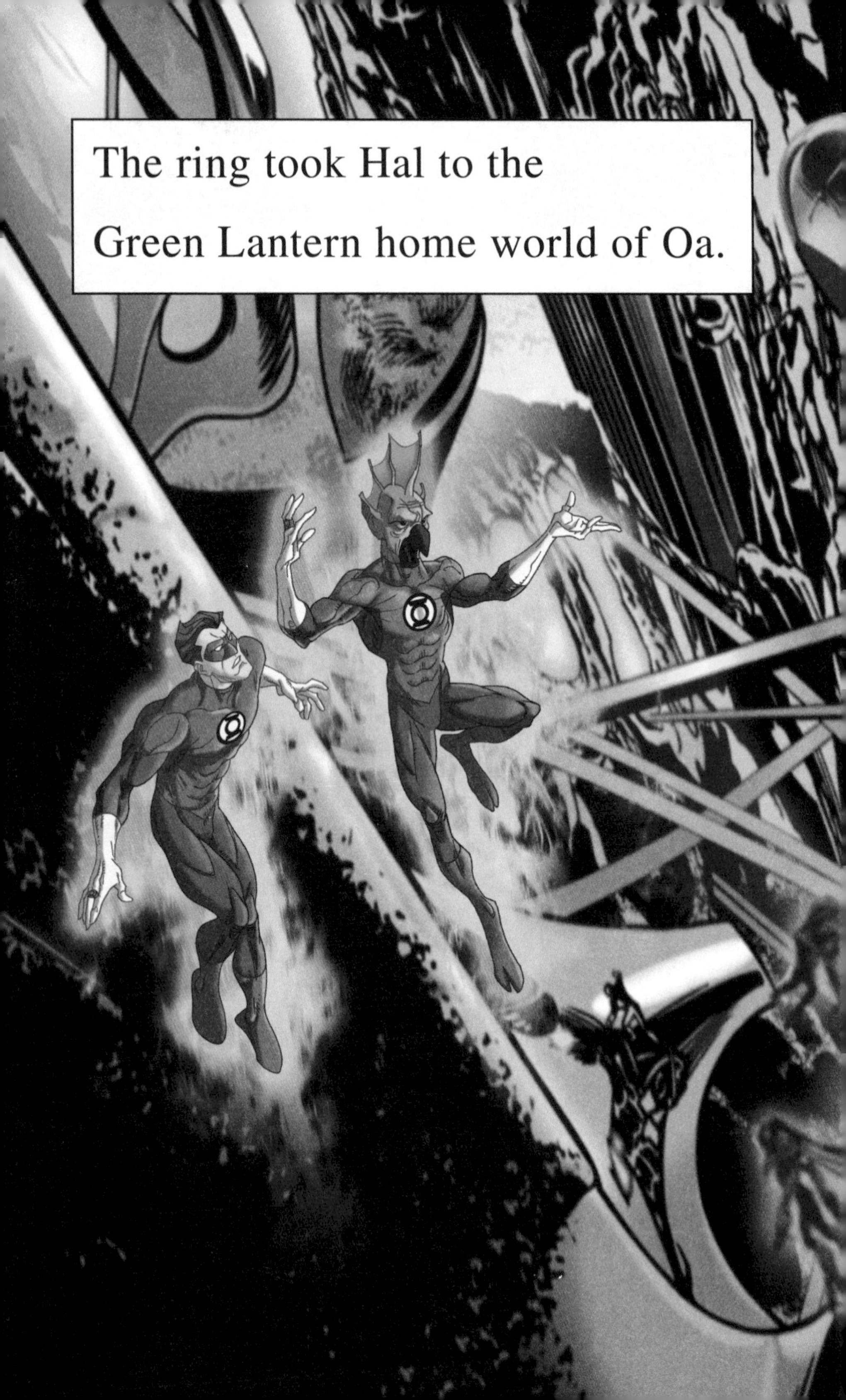

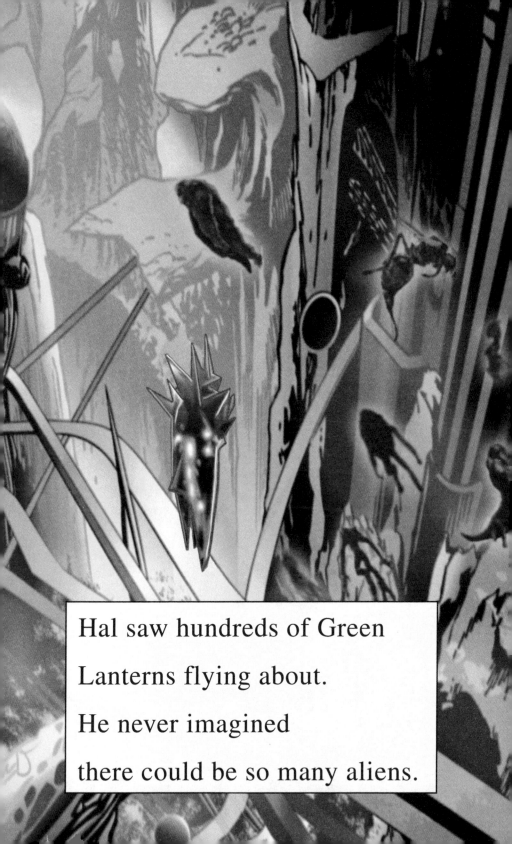

Hal saw hundreds of Green
Lanterns flying about.
He never imagined
there could be so many aliens.

To master his new powers,
Hal trained with a Green Lantern
named Kilowog.

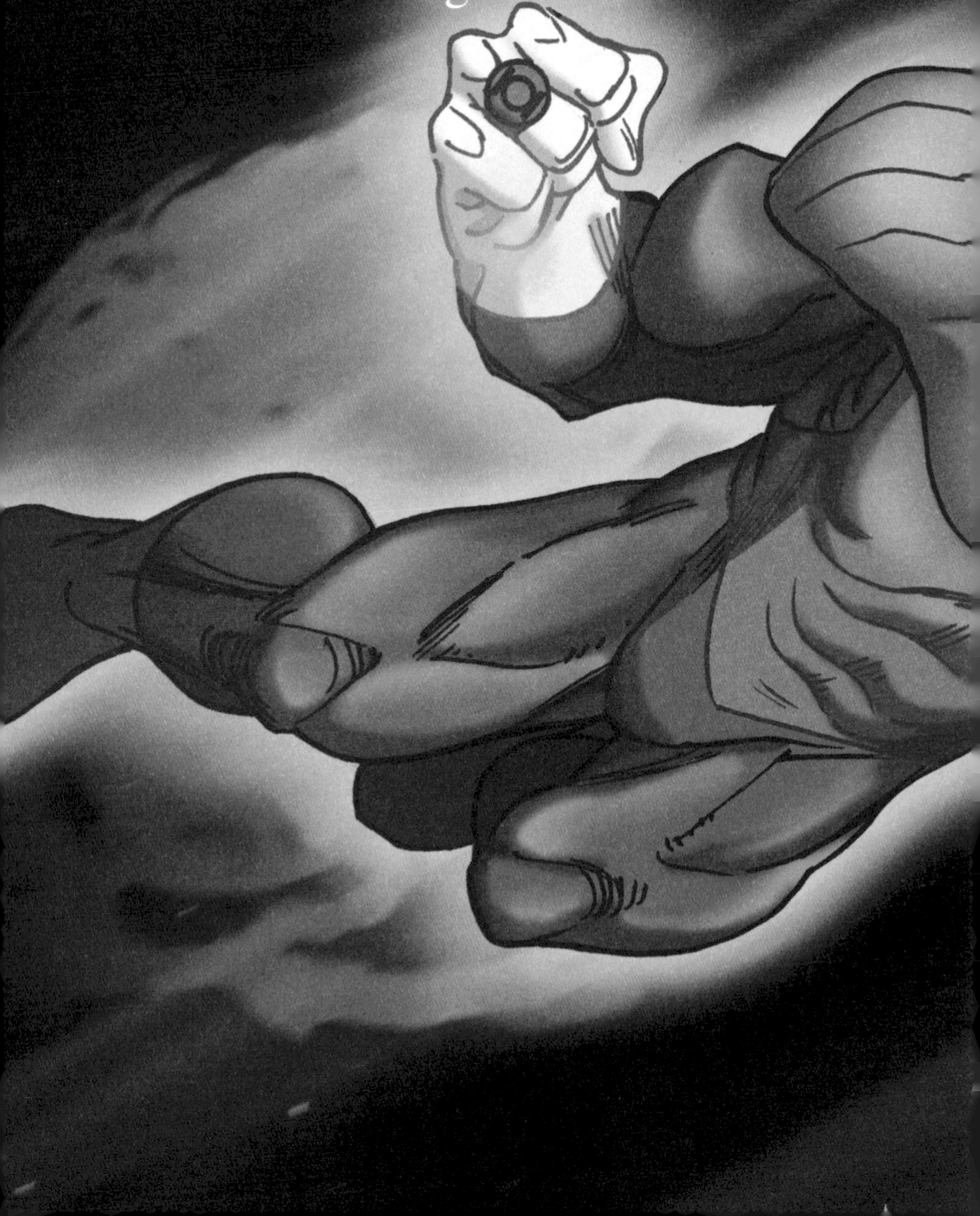

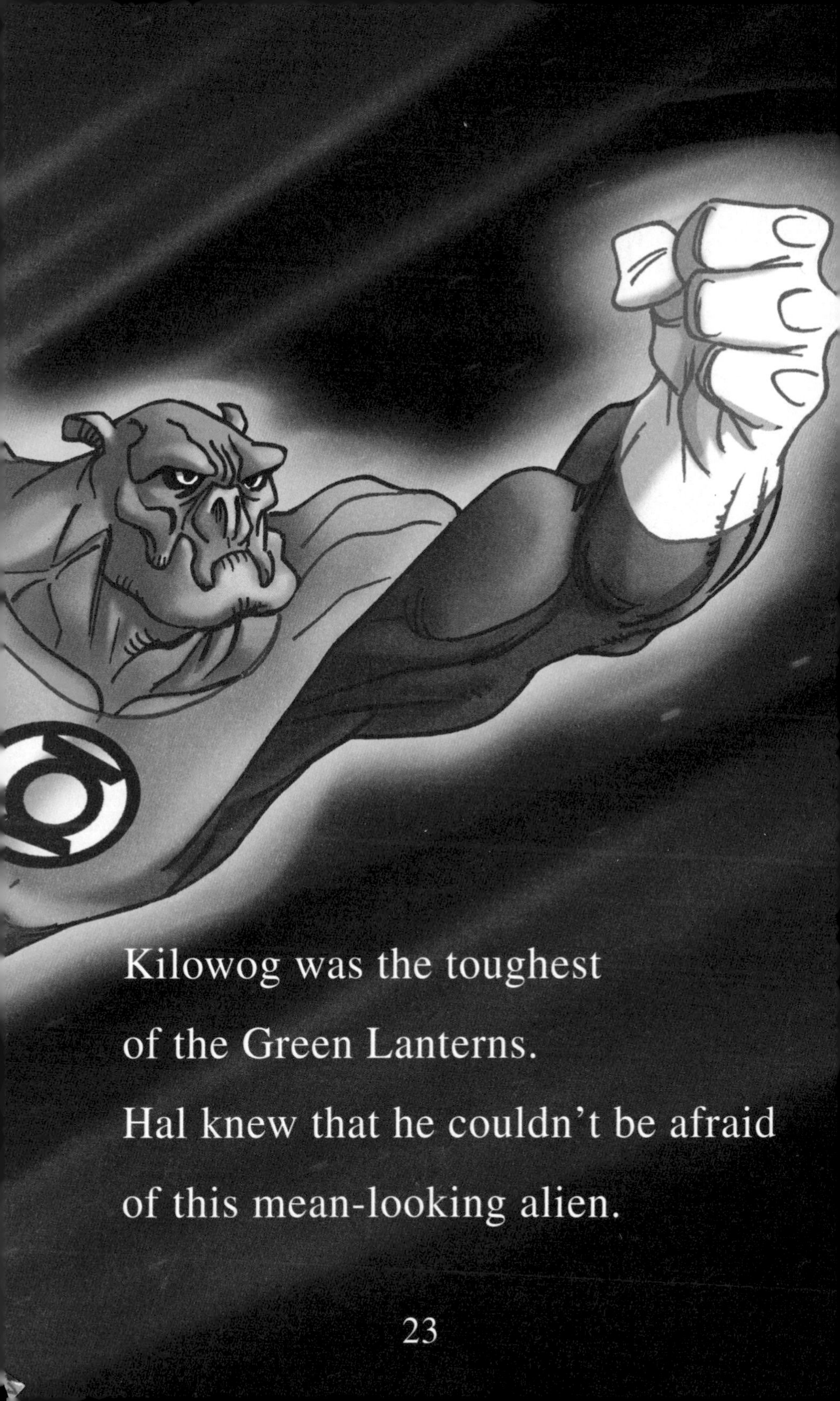

Kilowog was the toughest
of the Green Lanterns.
Hal knew that he couldn't be afraid
of this mean-looking alien.

It wasn't easy, but Hal overcame his fears and finished his training with Kilowog. He became an official member of the Green Lantern Corps.

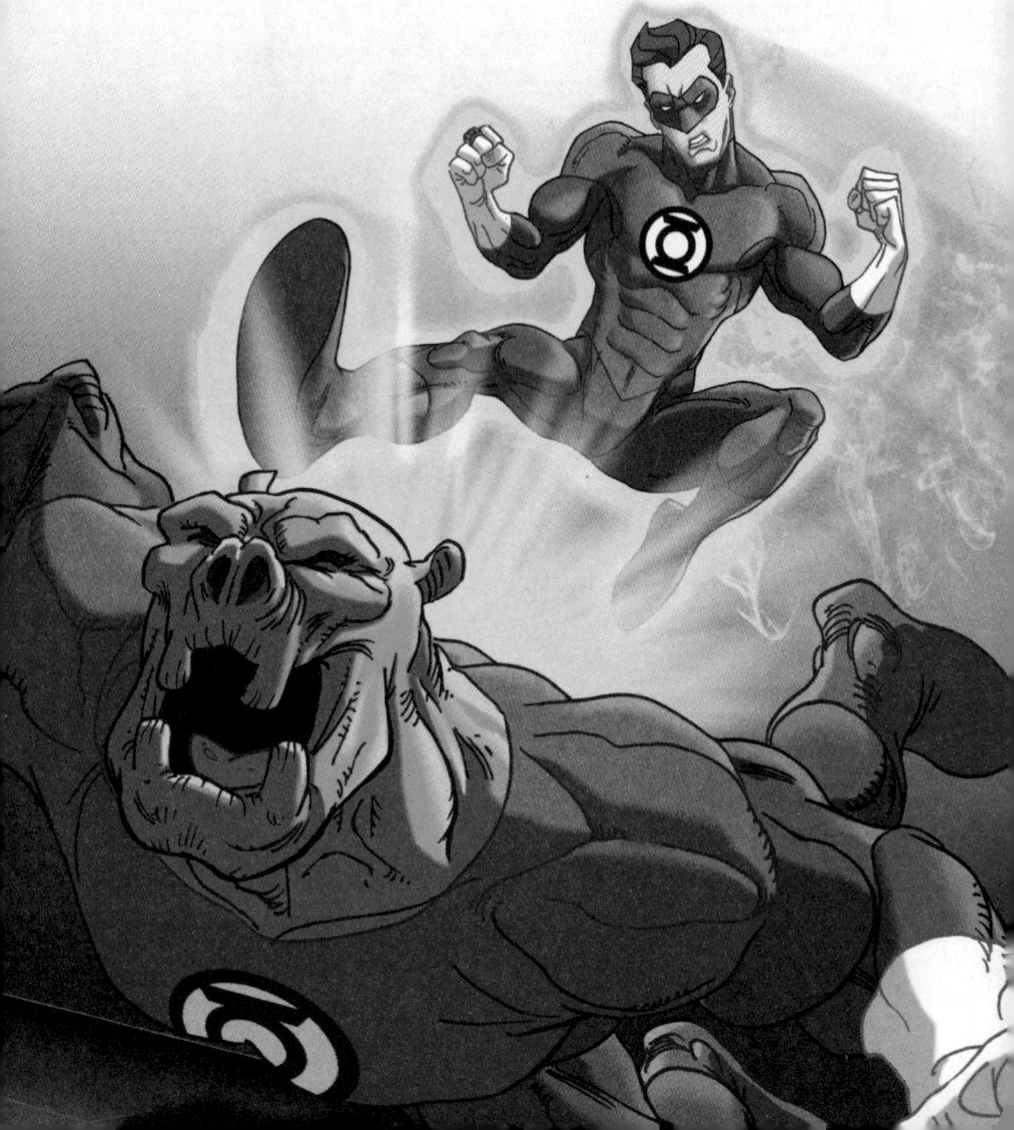

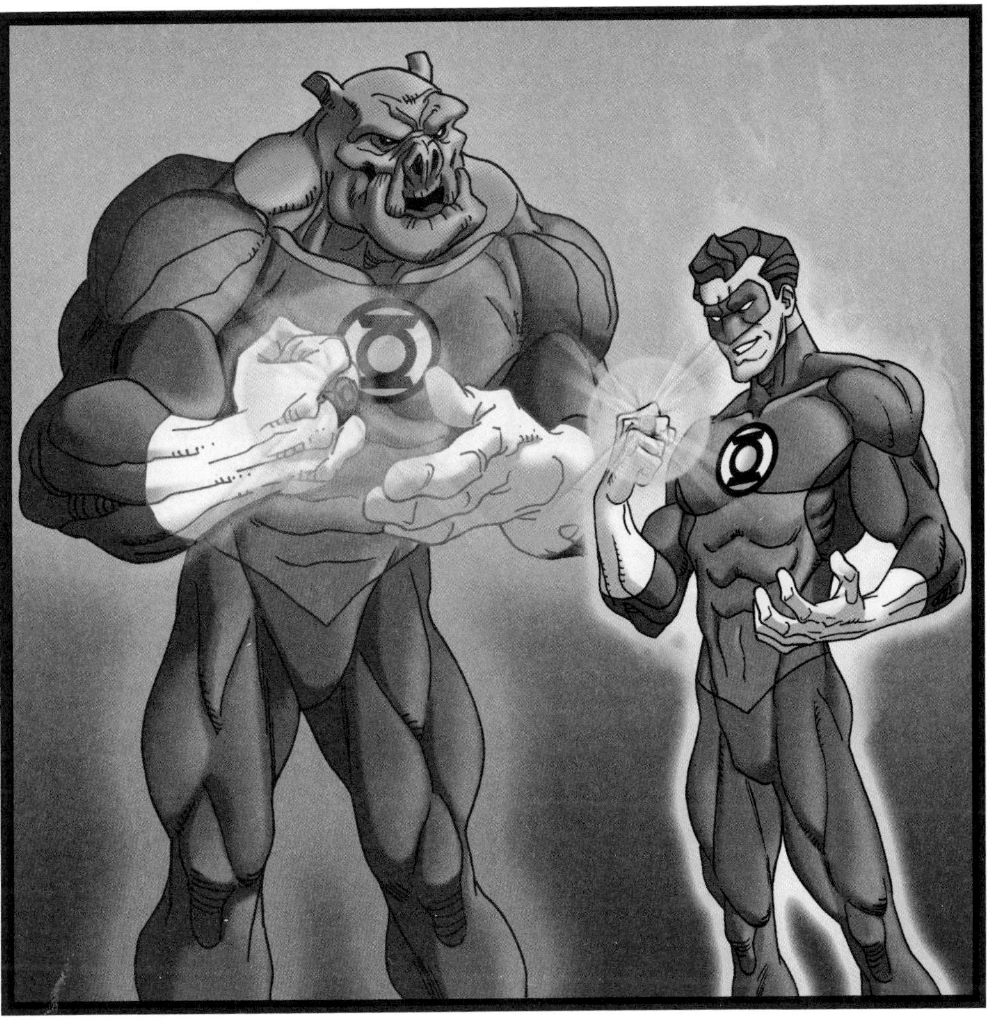

Using what Kilowog taught him,

Hal returned to Earth as its new protector.

No matter how tough an enemy was,

Hal was never scared.

With his new Green Lantern powers,
Hal joined the Justice League.
As a defender of Earth, he stood
alongside the World's Greatest Super Heroes.

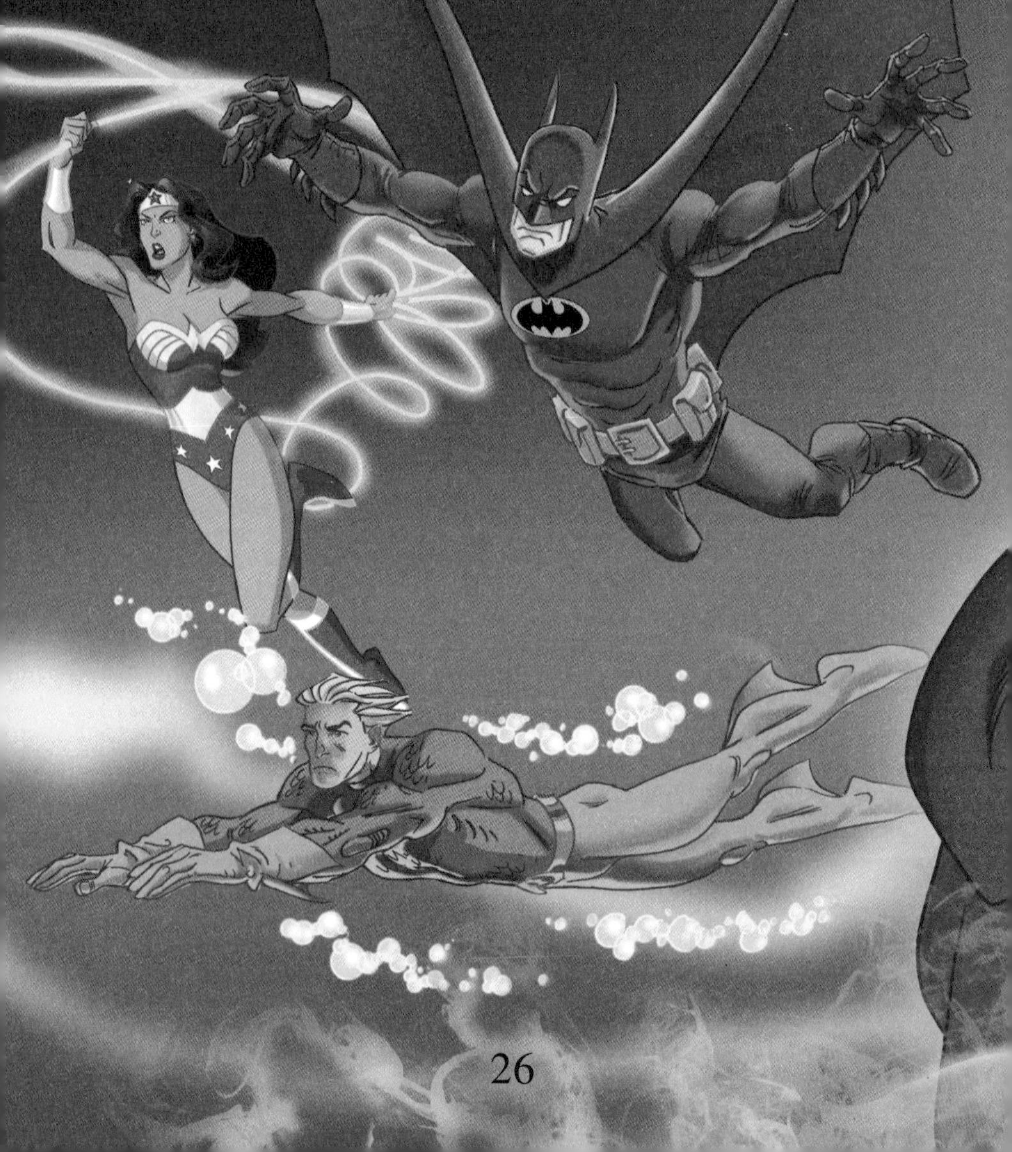

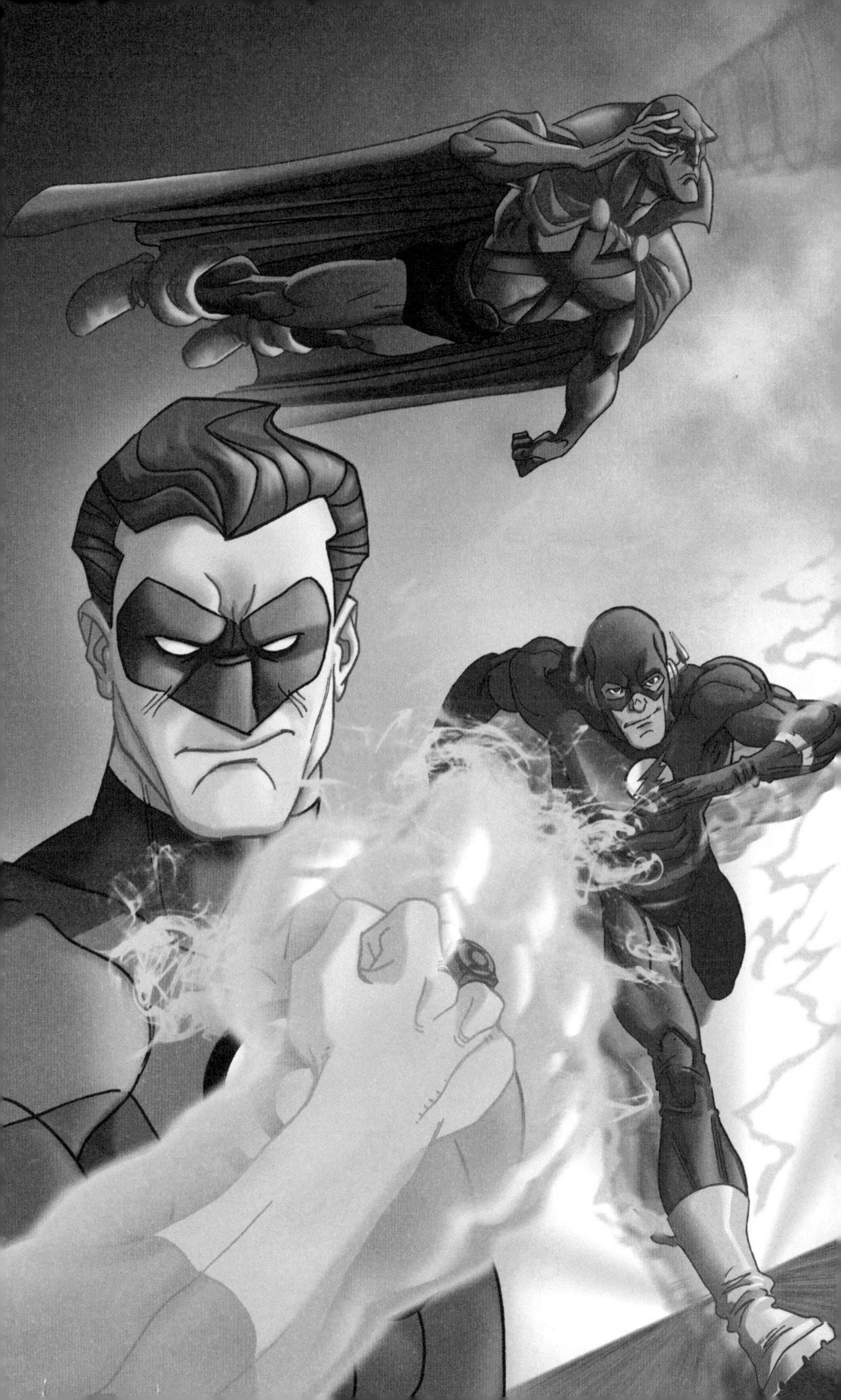

He teamed up with the Flash and Martian Manhunter to battle Sinestro.

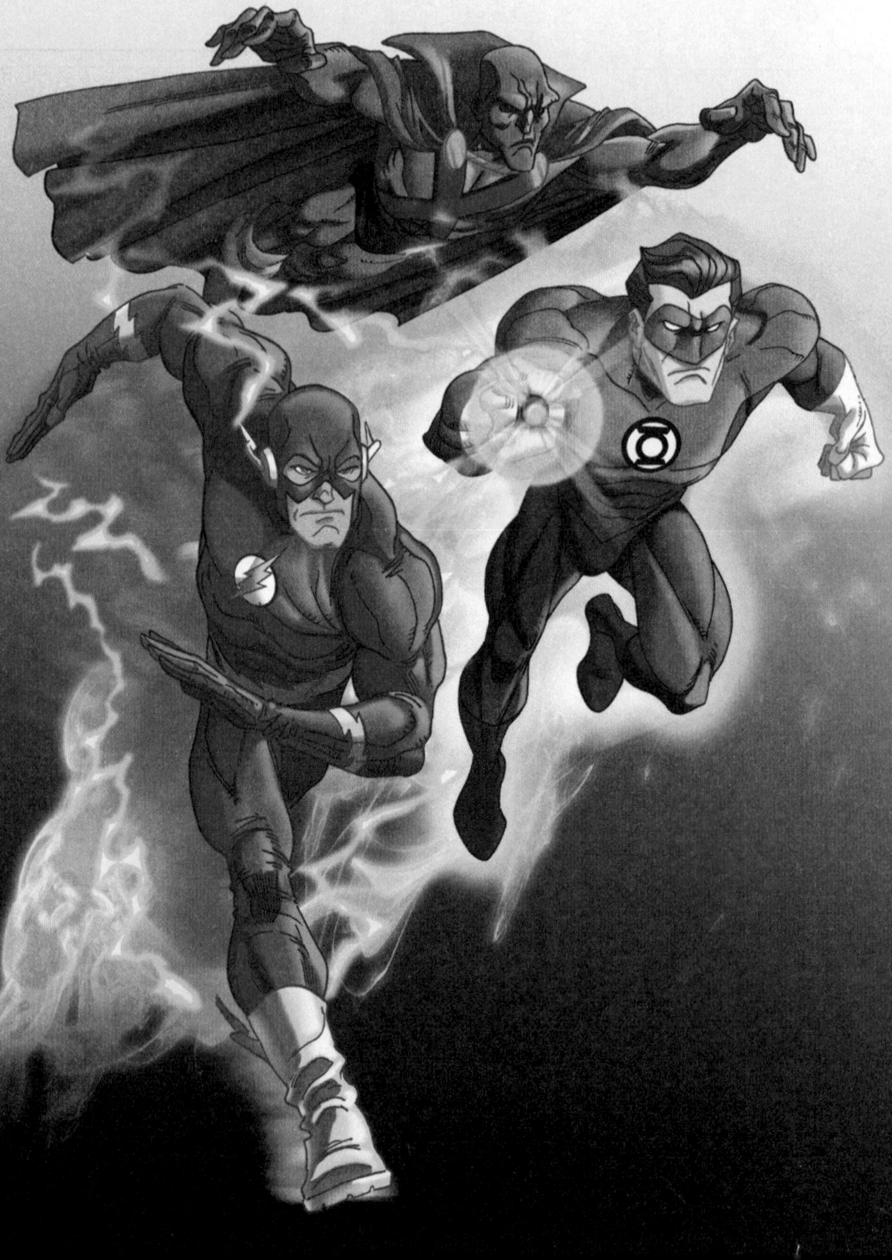

Sinestro was a former Green Lantern and was just as strong as Hal.

But he wasn't as strong as the combined power of the Justice League.

Like all great heroes, Hal knew that he was stronger with the help of his friends.

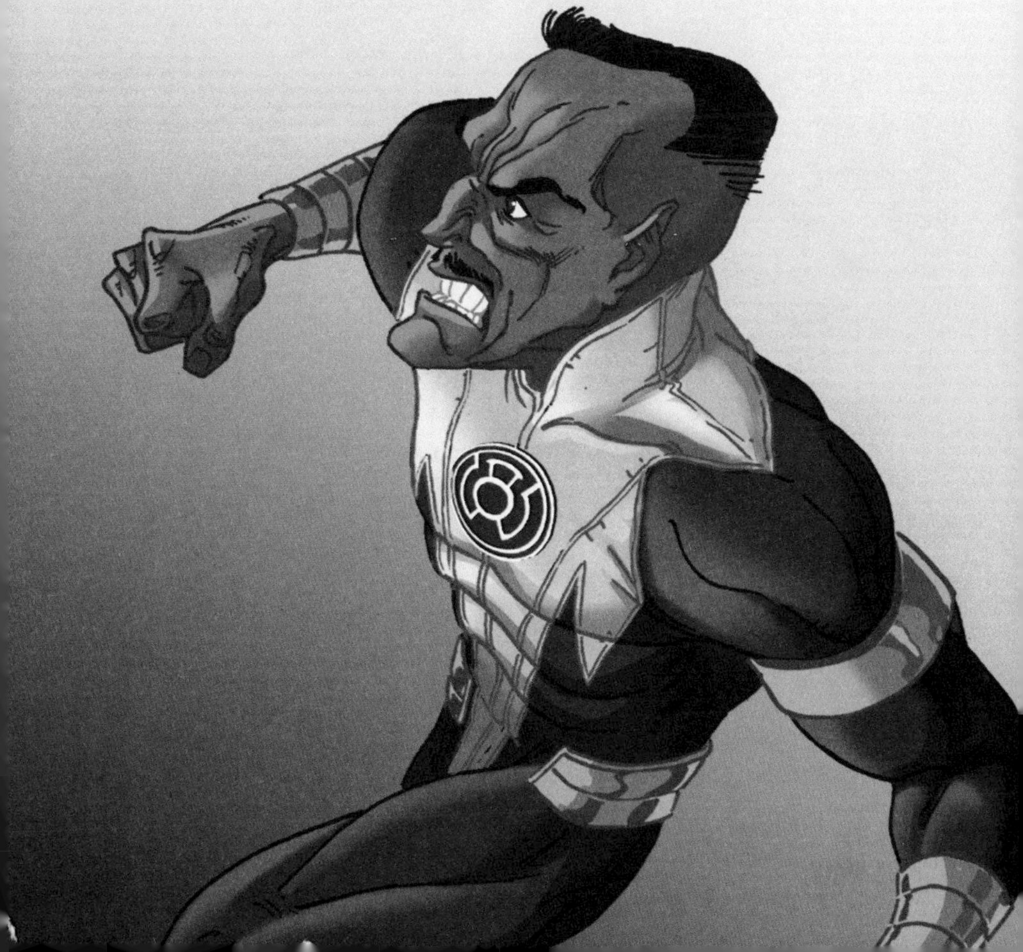

As Hal fought to defend Earth from countless villains, he always heard the Green Lantern oath in his head.

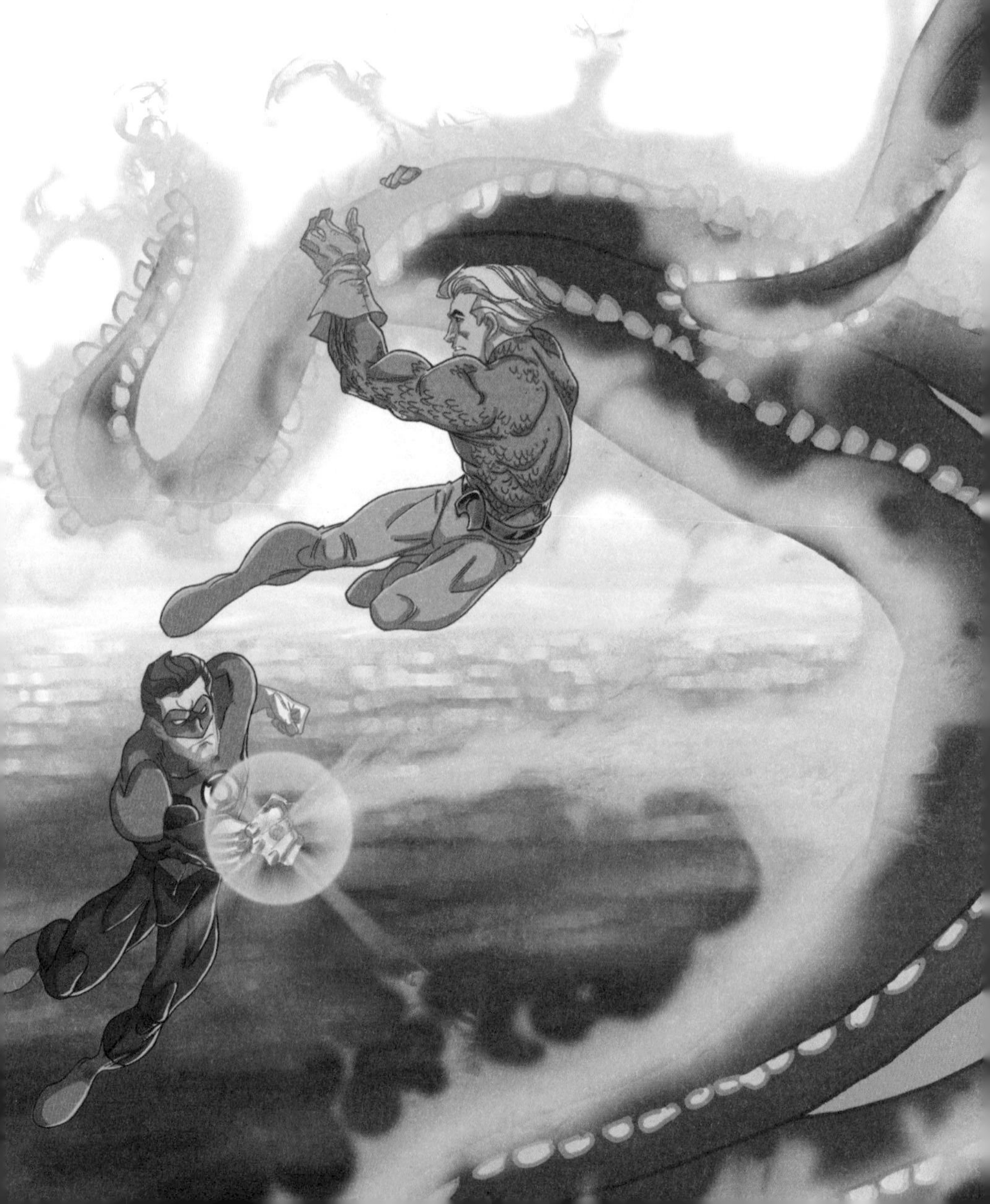

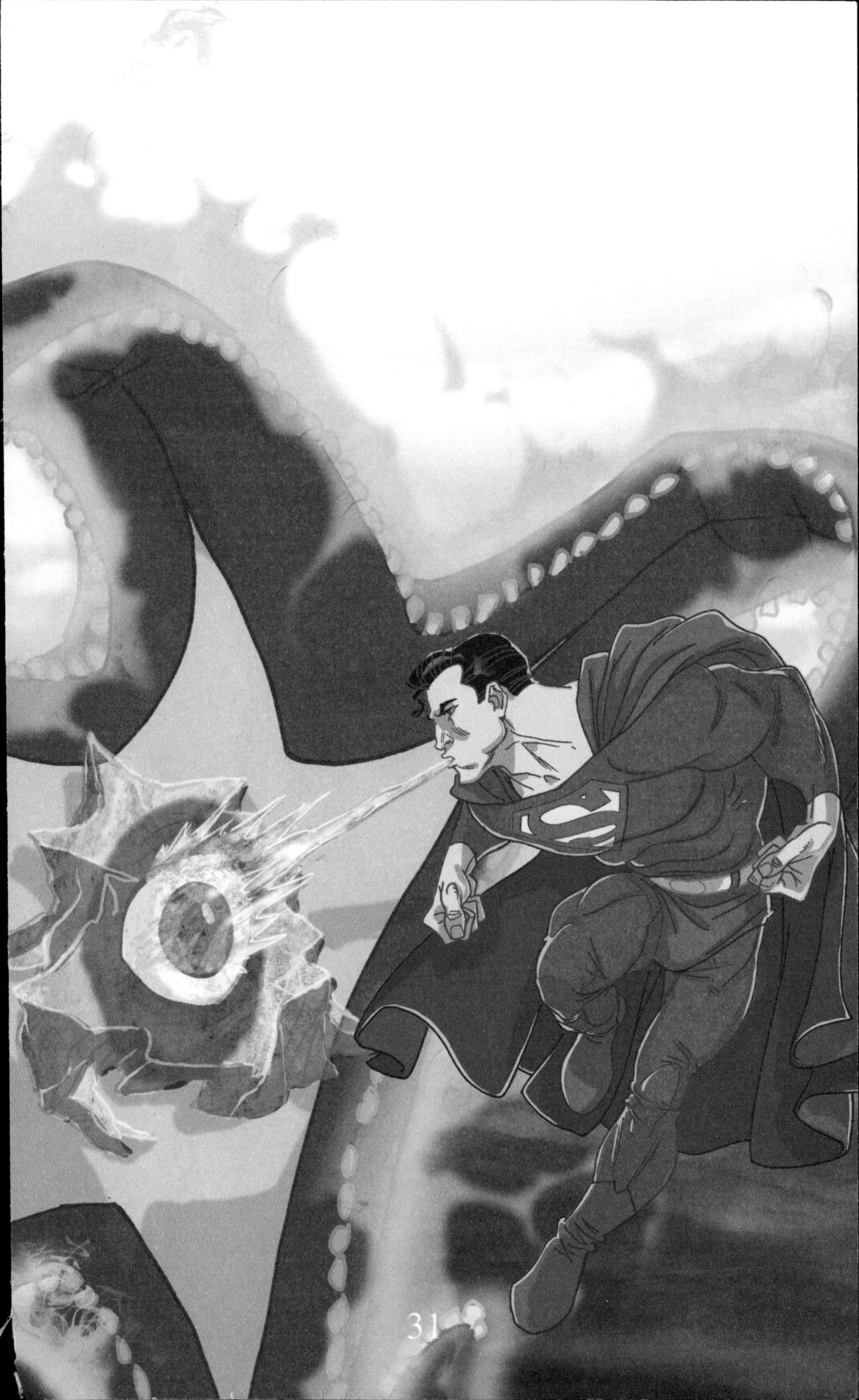

In brightest day, in blackest night,
no evil shall escape my sight.
Let those who worship evil's might
beware my power—Green Lantern's light!

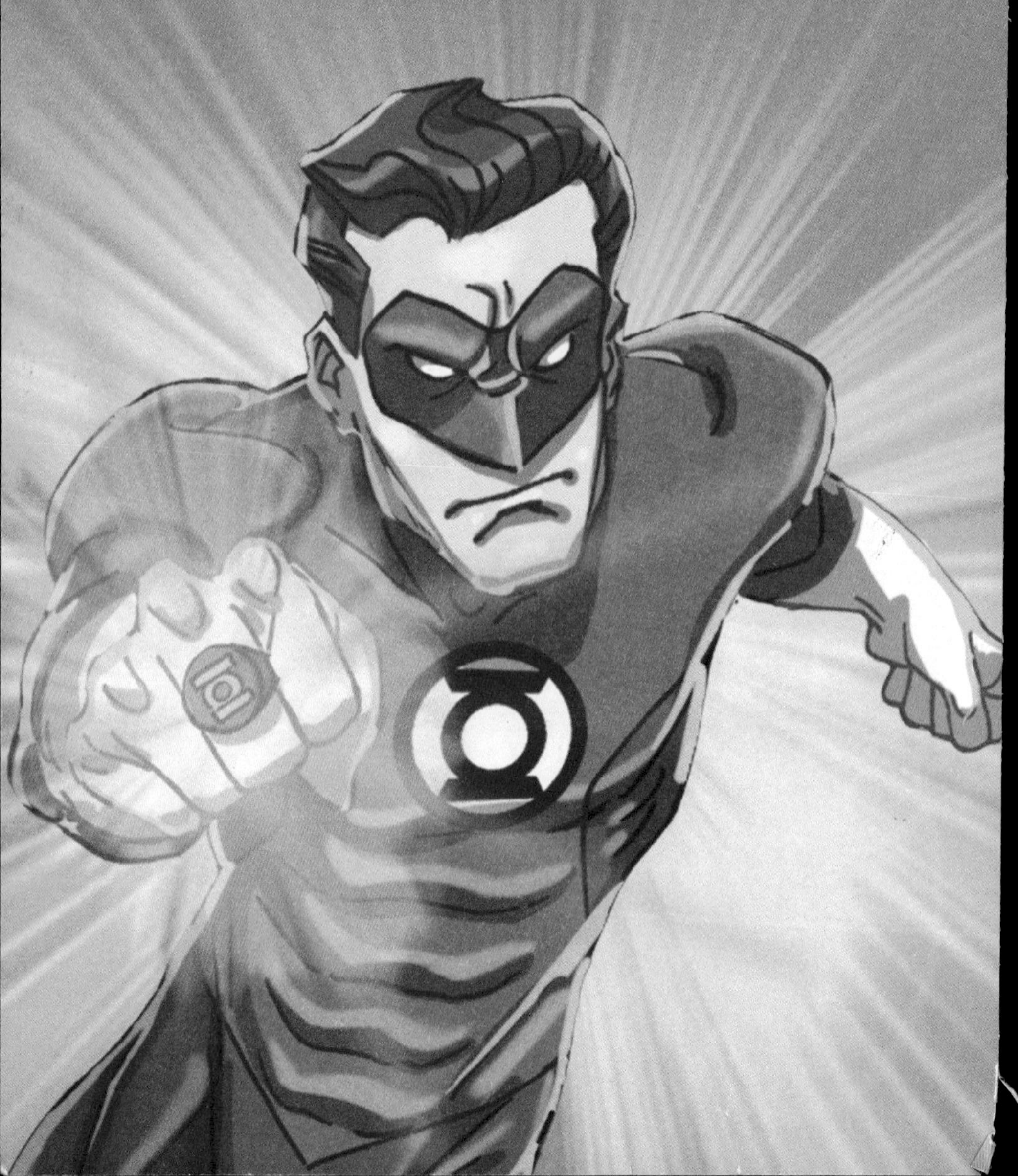